Famous Myths and Legends of the World

Myths and Legends of North America:
SOUTHWESTERN UNITED STATES AND MEXICO

WORLD BOOK

a Scott Fetzer company
Chicago
www.worldbook.com

World Book, Inc.
180 North LaSalle Street
Suite 900
Chicago, Illinois 60601
USA

For information about other World Book publications, visit our website at **www.worldbook.com** or call **1-800-967-5325.**

Library of Congress Cataloging-in-Publication Data

Myths and legends of North America: Southwestern United States and Mexico.
    pages cm. -- (Famous myths and legends of the world)
    Summary: "Myths and legends from the Southwest of the United States and Mexico. Features include information about the history and culture behind the myths, pronunciations, lists of deities, word glossary, further information, and index"--Provided by publisher.
    Includes index.
    ISBN 978-0-7166-2627-5
    1. Indians of North America--Southwest, New--Folklore--Juvenile literature. 2. Indians of Mexico--Folklore--Juvenile literature. 3. Indians of North America--Southwest, New--History--Juvenile literature. 4. Indians of Mexico--History--Juvenile literature. I. World Book, Inc. II. Series: Famous myths and legends of the world.
    E77.4.M98 2015
    398.2089'97--dc23

                                    2015014769

Set ISBN: 978-0-7166-2625-1
E-book ISBN: 978-0-7166-2639-8 (EPUB3)

Printed in China by PrintWORKS Global Services, Shenzhen, Guangdong
2nd printing May 2016

Writer: Scott A. Leonard

Staff for World Book, Inc.
Executive Committee
President: Jim O'Rourke
Vice President and Editor in Chief: Paul A. Kobasa
Vice President, Finance: Donald D. Keller
Vice President, Marketing: Jean Lin
Director, International Sales: Kristin Norell
Director, Licensing Sales: Edward Field
Director, Human Resources: Bev Ecker

Editorial
Manager, Annuals/Series Nonfiction: Christine Sullivan
Managing Editor, Annuals/Series Nonfiction:
    Barbara Mayes
Administrative Assistant: Ethel Matthews
Manager, Indexing Services: David Pofelski
Manager, Contracts & Compliance
    (Rights & Permissions): Loranne K. Shields

Manufacturing/Production
Manufacturing Manager: Sandra Johnson
Production/Technology Manager: Anne Fritzinger
Proofreader: Nathalie Strassheim

Graphics and Design
Senior Art Director: Tom Evans
Coordinator, Design Development and Production:
    Brenda Tropinski
Senior Designers: Matthew Carrington,
    Isaiah W. Sheppard, Jr.
Media Researcher: Jeff Heimsath
Manager, Cartographic Services: Wayne K. Pichler
Senior Cartographer: John M. Rejba

Staff for Brown Bear Books Ltd
Managing Editor: Tim Cooke
Editorial Director: Lindsey Lowe
Children's Publisher: Anne O'Daly
Design Manager: Keith Davis
Designer: Mike Davis
Picture Manager: Sophie Mortimer

CONTENTS

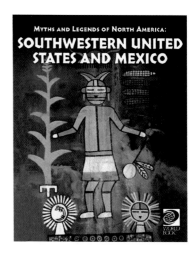

Muyingwa (MOO-ihng-wah), the Hopi god of germination, is portrayed in a mural by acclaimed Hopi artist Fred Kabotie. The mural can be found at the Desert View Watchtower on the South Rim at Grand Canyon National Park in Arizona.

© Tom Bean, Corbis Images

Note to Readers:

Phonetic pronunciations have been inserted into the myths and legends in this volume to make reading the stories easier and to give the reader some of the flavor of the cultures of the Southwest and Mexico the stories represent. See page 64 for a pronunciation key.

The myths and legends retold in this volume are written in a creative way to provide an engaging reading experience and approximate the artistry of the originals. Many of these stories were not written down but were recited by storytellers from generation to generation. Even when some of the stories came to be written down they likely did not feature phonetic pronunciations for challenging names and words! We hope the inclusion of this material will improve rather than distract from your experience of the stories.

Some of the figures mentioned in the myths and legends in this volume are described on page 60 in the section "Deities of Southwestern United States and Mexico." In addition, some unusual words in the text are defined in the Glossary on page 62.

INTRODUCTION

The World of the Pueblo Indians, page 29

Since the earliest times, people have told stories to try to explain the world in which they lived. These stories are known as myths. Myths try to answer these kinds of questions: How was the world created? Who were the first people? Where did the animals come from? Why does the sun rise and set? Why is the land devastated by storms or drought? Today, people often rely on science to answer many of these questions. But in earlier times—and in some parts of the world today—people explained natural events using stories about gods, goddesses, spirits of nature, and heroes.

Myths are different from folk tales and legends. Folk tales are fictional stories about animals or human beings. Most of these tales are not set in any particular time or place, and they begin and end in a certain way. For example, many English folk tales begin with the phrase "Once upon a time" and end with "They lived happily ever after." Legends are set in the real world, in the present or the historical past. Legends distort the truth, but they are based on real people or events.

Myths, in contrast, typically tell of events that have taken place in the remote past. Unlike legends, myths have also played—and often continue to play—an important role in a society's religious life. Although legends may have religious themes, most are not religious in nature. The people of a society may tell folk tales and legends for amusement, without believing them. But they usually consider their myths sacred and completely true. Most myths concern *divinities* (divine beings) that have powers far greater than those of any human being. At the same time, however, many gods, goddesses, and heroes of mythology have human characteristics. They are guided by such emotions as love and jealousy, and they may experience birth and death. A number of mythological figures even look like human beings. In many cases, the human qualities of the divinities reflect a society's ideals. Good gods and goddesses have the qualities a society admires, and evil ones have the qualities it dislikes. In myths, the actions of these divinities influence the world of humans for better or for worse.

The World of the Cochiti Pueblo, pages 32-33

Myths can sometimes seem very strange. They sometimes seem to take place in a world that is both like our world and unlike it. Time can go backward and forward, so it is sometimes difficult to tell in what order events happen. People may be dead and alive at the same time.

Myths were originally passed down from generation to generation by word of mouth. Partly for this reason, there are often different versions of the same story.

In early times, every society developed its own myths, though many myths across cultures share similar themes, such as a battle between good and evil. The myths of a society generally reflect the landscape, climate, and society in which the storytellers lived.

Myths tell a people about their distant history and why the society is structured in the way it is. They show people how to behave in the world and find their way. As teaching tools, myths help to prepare children for their lives as adults.

Myths of the Southwest and Mexico

Before the arrival of Europeans in the Americas, the desert southwest of what is now the United States was the homeland of numerous peoples. Some of these people were farmers who lived in settled communities we know as pueblos. Other Native American peoples were nomads who hunted wild animals and gathered food and moved with the seasons.

Numerous Native American groups lived in what are now the southwestern United States or Mexico.

For all of these peoples, religion was a central element of life. Among the Pueblo people, religious leaders governed the villages. Although there was no single Native American religion, certain beliefs were widespread. Most important was the belief in a mysterious force in nature that was superior to human beings and capable of influencing their lives. Most Indians believed that the spirit power could be gained by certain people or through certain ceremonies. Such ceremonies were held to ask the spirits to ensure abundant game and provide sufficient rain for their crops. Another common Indian belief was that of a guardian spirit who helped guide a person through the hardships of life.

The World of the Aztec warriors, page 54

Modern-day Mexico was the home of a number of powerful empires, including the Toltec, Zapotec, Maya, and especially the Aztec. These groups worshiped many gods. The Aztec developed one of the most interesting mythologies in the Americas because they borrowed many of their divinities from earlier Indian cultures as well as the neighboring peoples they conquered. The Aztec as well as almost every Indian civilization in Mexico worshiped the god Quetzalcoatl (keht sahl koh WAH tuhl), whom the Aztec associated with the arts.

Religious ceremonies and festivals dominated the lives of the ancient peoples of Mexico. In some cultures, these events included human sacrifice. The Aztec believed their gods required a constant supply of human blood to maintain order.

By examining myths, we can better understand the feelings and values that bind members of society into one group. We can compare the myths of various cultures to discover how these cultures differ and how they resemble one another. We can also study myths to try to understand why people behave as they do.

How Coyote Brought
FIRE TO THE

The Apache tell this story to explain how the people came to have such a useful tool to keep them warm, provide light, and cook food.

In the first days, back when animals and plants still talked, only the Firefly people had fire. Tall rocks surrounded their camp, and there was no trail down to it. Coyote the Trickster paced the rocks above. But even one so clever as he could not find a path down to the camp. Then, one day, he saw some Firefly children at the base of the rocks, playing the hoop-and-pole game.

Coyote used some berries to make necklaces and threw them down to the children. He asked them, "Tell me where I can find the trail down to the Firefly camp."

The children hesitated but eventually they gave him the directions. "By the edge of the rocks is a cedar tree. If you take hold of its branches, the tree will bend and lower you to the ground below. Then if someone says to it, 'Bend down to me,' it will bend down and take him from that place."

Coyote gathered enough cedar bark to make a torch and rode the tree down to the Firefly camp. Some folks were playing a game, betting their hides (skin) on the outcome. The losers had their hides stripped from them; but, after they jumped into the river and climbed out, they had a hide as before.

Coyote asked if he could join in; he wanted to bet his hide on the game. The other players said, "No, your hide sticks too closely to your nose. If we strip it off, you will cry too much."

But eventually, the people agreed to let him play. And, of course, he lost. And, of course, he cried terribly when they pulled his hide off.

Near sundown, the Firefly people built a fire and prepared to dance. Coyote tied the bundle of cedar bark to his tail and joined the celebration. He danced wildly, close to the fire.

"Your tail is on fire!" cried the Firefly people. "I'm working magic with it," replied Coyote. "It won't burn."

Suddenly, Coyote the Trickster dashed from the Firefly camp, his tail ablaze. "Bend down to me!" he shouted at the cedar tree. Before the Firefly people could stop him, Coyote was over the rock wall, running flat out, with his burning tail whipping from side to side. Soon the whole world was on fire.

The trees kept the fire. That is why, to this day, wood burns. It keeps Coyote's gift.

The World of THE APACHE

There are several Apache (uh PACH ee) nations—the Lipan (lih PAHN), Mescalero (mehs kuh LAIR oh), and Jicarilla (hee kuh REE yuh). The original Jicarilla homeland was the area between what are now the Sangre de Cristo (SAHN-gray day KREE-stoh) Mountains and the plains of southern Colorado and northern New Mexico, in the southwestern United States.

The Apache were fierce fighters who sometimes raided the settlements of the neighboring Pueblo people. The Apache did some farming but chiefly relied on hunting animals and gathering wild plants for their food. They did not have permanent houses, living in brush shelters or tipis. In the late 1800's, the Apache became known for their resistance to U.S. government attempts to keep them on reservations.

The Jicarilla Apache, such as Allenroy Paquin (right), keep their traditional culture alive by performing dances and telling stories. Paquin is also a skilled silversmith and beadworker.

FIERCE FIGHTERS

The Apache built sweat lodges (left) from willow branches covered in skins or *adobe* (dried mud). They poured water over heated rocks inside the lodge to release steam, which caused the occupants to perspire. The Apache believed sweat lodge ceremonies purified the body, cured illness, and influenced the spirits.

AN APACHE GAME

Many Native American peoples play a version of the hoop-and-pole game mentioned in "How Coyote Brought Fire to the People." The basic game requires three players: one to roll the hoop and two competitors to throw poles (long sticks) through it. Most hoops feature some sort of webbing—made of string, buckskin laces, or corn stalks—with a small hole at the center. Scoring depends on whether the pole passes through the hoop or merely strikes it.

Saguaro cactuses rise from rocky hills bordering the Apache Trail, a pathway through the Superstition Mountains in Arizona.

The Apache believed that families were very important. Families were responsible for making sure that traditional stories and knowledge would be passed down to the following generations.

THE ORIGIN OF

The Zuni tell this myth to explain the origin of corn, which has traditionally been their main food and the basis of their lifestyle.

In the days when Earth was new, soon after the first people issued from Earth-Mother, the Twin-Brothers-of-Light, who were the sons of the Sun-Father, gave the people powerful gifts for healing and long life. The first tribes were named according to the gifts they received.

The Bear and Crane peoples received the secrets of snow and hail of winter. With this knowledge, they also received the medicine seeds necessary to heal the sicknesses of winter. The Eagle, Deer, and Coyote peoples were entrusted with the "Medicine Deer Seed." From this seed descended the hunting bands whose skill fed the people.

The Frog peoples received the "Medicine Seed of Water" and the sacred dance. Without this seed, all of Earth would dry up. Even the insects of the mountains and hollows would die of thirst.

To the Badger peoples were entrusted the secrets of fire. In the roots of all trees—which the burrowing Badger can find—is the source of fire, a power the Zuni draw from Earth-Mother.

The Twin-Brothers-of-Light gave the Seed peoples of the Zuni the "Medicine Seed of Corn." This seed is the parent of flesh and beauty, the solace of hunger, and the emblems of birth, mortal life, death, and immortality.

"Go," the Twin-Brothers-of-Light told the Seed peoples. "You must wander for many generations toward the East until at last you come to the middle of the world. There your children will dwell in the embrace of Earth-Mother until the sun grows dark."

And so the Seed peoples traveled, always moving east. They hunted game for their flesh-food and gathered grass

CORN

seeds for their bread-food, and bound rushes about them for their clothing. In those days, the land was filled with stranger-beings and monsters that preyed upon the people.

"The people, our children, are less fortunate than the monsters," said the Twin-Brothers-of-Light. "For to every beast is given strength or some form of wisdom, but the people have only the power of guessing."

One day, the Twin-Brothers-of-Light gathered the people and the plant-eating animals together. They laid their water shield upon the ground and placed a thunderbolt facing each of the four directions. When all was ready, they let fly the lightning. And as soft clay is turned to rock in the fire, so the monsters were transformed in a moment to everlasting rock. One may still behold their twisted forms along every mountainside and ravine. But the Twins spared a few predators so that Earth would not overflow with the living and bring all to starvation.

The Seed peoples of the Zuni finally came to the Place of Misty Waters. But stranger-beings, who also called themselves the Seed people, already lived there. The Zuni challenged the stranger-beings: "How is it you take on the name and attributes of our clan?"

"We have power with the highest gods," the stranger-beings replied. "But we cannot use it without your help."

To settle matters, they held a contest. For eight days the Seed peoples of the Zuni gathered sticks and the feathers of summer birds, planting them to waft their prayers to heaven. In answer to

their prayers, a great rain fell, bringing with it rich new soil.

"See," said the Zuni clans. "We have prevailed. Our power has brought forth water and new soil."

"This is good," said the stranger-beings. "But you did not bring forth life." And they set off in their turn, dancing and singing for eight days.

"Behold!" the stranger-beings cried. And where the Zuni Seed clan had planted plumed sticks, there were now seven stalks of corn, heavy with ripened grain their tassels waving in the wind.

"These stalks," said the stranger-beings, "arise from the flesh of our own sisters and daughters. The eldest sister is the yellow corn; the next, the blue; the next, the red; the next, the white; the next,

the speckled; and the next, the black. The last and youngest is the sweet-corn, who is soft like all the young."

"Are we not brothers?" asked the stranger-beings. "We are indeed!" replied the Zuni. "Should we not travel together to the middle of the world?"

"This we will do," declared the stranger-beings. "From now on, you will not eat grass seeds, but the corn-flesh of our maidens. And we will drink your water. You will plant your prayer-plumes. We will dance and sing with our maidens so all may prosper."

And so together they traveled. The Seed clans joined to become the Corn Clan, or the people. At last, they reached their journey's end at the heart of Earth-Mother, which is Shi-wi-na-kwin, or the "Land of the Zuni."

The World of THE ZUNI

The Zuni (ZOON yee or ZOO nee) Indians are a Pueblo Indian tribe living in west-central New Mexico, near the border with Arizona, in the southwestern United States. Most Zuni live on the Zuni Indian Reservation, which the tribe has inhabited for thousands of years. The Zuni are descended from a prehistoric group sometimes called the Anasazi (AH nuh SAH zee) or Ancestral Puebloans. Many Zuni continue to practice their traditional religion through dances, prayer sticks, and various celebrations, much as their ancestors did.

Traditionally dressed Zuni dancers participate in a parade during an annual fair on the Zuni Tribal Reservation.

Zuni Point (right in photo) is a lookout along the south rim of the Grand Canyon in Arizona. According to myth, the Zuni people began at a site known as Ribbon Falls on Bright Angel Creek, which flows to the Colorado River from the north rim of the Grand Canyon.

SACRED CORN

Native peoples throughout what is now the southwestern United States and Central America told myths about the origin of corn, which is also known as maize. The stories reflected the importance of corn in an environment where wheat and other grain crops did not thrive. Corn was eaten from cobs as well as milled into flour that was used to make different forms of bread. Most native peoples believed that corn was a gift from the gods.

Zuni crops grow in walled fields, in a woodcut from the 1800's. Archaeological records indicate that the Zuni have farmed and raised livestock with the aid of irrigation ditches in what is now western New Mexico for about 3,000 years.

WISE-SON

and the Grand Canyon

The Hopi tell this myth to explain the origin of the Snake Ceremony and the role of the Vision Quest in the spiritual education of young men.

Wise-Son meditated on the rim of a huge canyon, imagining where the mighty river below came to an end. None of the tribal elders could answer his question for him. So Wise-Son approached his father, saying, "It is time that I undertook my quest. I wish to discover where the mighty river has its end."

The people of his village helped Wise-Son. They built a boat, sealed tight like a cocoon. Wise-Son fashioned a special pushing pole to guide his boat. The village shaman placed prayer sticks on the pole, blessing Wise-Son's journey.

Wise-Son traveled for many weeks, passing through dangerous rapids and floating through dark tunnels. One day, Wise-Son noticed the river had become salty. Then he found himself in endless open water. The river ended in the Ocean-Where-the-Sun-Sleeps.

In the distance, he saw an island, so he steered toward it. Coming ashore, he saw a house with a tiny door. Wise-Son called out, "May I come in?" A voice replied, "Make the door large enough, then enter."

Wise-Son did so. Inside he found Spider-Woman. He presented her with one of his prayer sticks and told her of his long journey. "When I return to my people, I wish to bring gifts that will help them." "There is a lodge nearby," Spider-Woman said. "The people in the lodge have many beautiful beads and rocks that could be suitable gifts. But I warn you, there are many dangerous beasts on the path to this lodge. I will give you a magic ointment for protection. I will perch on your ear and guide you."

A vast marsh blocked the way to the treasure lodge. Wise-Son poured some of the magical ointment over the ground and a rainbow bridge appeared overhead to guide them.

First, they came upon a lion baring its terrible teeth. Wise-Son tossed one of his prayer sticks to the beast and poured more of the ointment on the ground. The lion became calm. Going on, they met a huge bear, a wild-eyed cat, a monstrous wolf, and an enormous snake with a rattle and angry eyes. Each time, Wise-Son poured magic ointment on the ground and the creatures grew still.

Inside the treasure lodge, Wise-Son saw men squatting around the inner walls, wearing colorful beads and face paint. Wise-Son sat, remaining quiet for a long time. The men stared at him. At last, the chief got up, lit his pipe, and smoked four times. He handed the pipe to Wise-Son, who smoked the pipe the magic number of times. Pleased, the chief and his men greeted Wise-Son warmly. Wise-Son gave each of them a prayer stick.

"Now we must put on our snakeskins," said the chief. "Turn away! Do not observe how we do this." Wise-Son obeyed. In his ear, Spider-Woman said, "They will not harm you, only frighten you. Be strong and do as I tell you!"

When Wise-Son turned around, the men were gone and the floor was writhing with hissing and rattling snakes. The chief spoke to Wise-Son, "If you can choose which is my daughter, we will show you our ceremonial dance and give you many beads and precious stones for your people."

Wise-Son heard Spider-Woman's voice in his ear, "Choose the yellow snake with rattles." Wise-Son did so, and the yellow snake became a beautiful young woman!

"I could fall in love with her," Wise-Son thought to himself.

As promised, the chief and other members of the Snake Clan taught Wise-Son all the secrets of the Snake Ceremony—the special words of thanksgiving, the special steps of the Snake Dance, the wearing of the Snake Skin, and the parts of the sacred altar.

After he had learned all he needed to know, Wise-Son and Spider-Woman returned to her house. He gave her another prayer stick. She gave him a small turquoise, a white shell, a red bead, and a large turquoise. She also gave him a large bag with many special beads to take to his people. "But," she said, "Do not open this bag until you reach your village."

Wise-Son returned to the treasure lodge to say good-bye. The chief said, "You have gained our friendship. Take my daughter as your wife."

The happy couple traveled for many moons. The bag Spider-Woman gave them grew heavier each day. Finally, they could resist their curiosity no longer and opened the bag. They strung beads together and put them around their necks. But the next morning, all the beads had vanished.

When Wise-Son at last returned, his people rejoiced and made his wife feel welcome. He told them where the river ends. He showed them the secrets of the Snake Ceremony. To this day, the Hopi Snake Clan proudly performs this ceremony so others may see the wonderful things the people at the end of the river showed Wise-Son.

The World of THE HOPI

The Hopi (HOH pee) Indians are one of the Pueblo Indian tribes. Many Hopi live in 11 villages in Arizona, in the southwestern United States, on or near three high *mesas* (hills or mountains with flat tops). One village, Oraibi, is one of the oldest continuously inhabited villages in the United States. It was founded about 800 years ago.

Hopi Indians dance with poisonous rattlesnakes in their mouths during the Snake Ceremony, in an illustration from 1908. The Hopi continue to hold the ceremony today, every two years at the end of August, as the climax of a 16-day period of prayer for rain. The Hopi believe that their ancestors came from underground and they consider snakes to be their brothers. They believe the snakes will carry their prayers for rain to the Rainmakers beneath Earth. The snakes are released unharmed after the ceremony.

A Hopi Indian on a burro surveys the land from the edge of a mesa.

A necklace of blue-green turquoise (TUR koyz) and red coral decorates the chest of a Hopi man, in a colored photograph from the 1920's. Turquoise, a mineral that occurs naturally in the Southwest, has long been prized for its beauty. The Hopi, Navajo, Apache, and other Native Americans of the Southwest have traditionally believed that turquoise can protect the body from sickness. According to Hopi tradition, Earth freed itself from the water that once covered it thanks to the ability of turquoise to hold back floods.

Hopi have traditionally held spiritual ceremonies in partially underground chambers called kivas (KEE vuhz), such as the one shown above. The sanctuaries are entered by a ladder through the roof. Modern kivas are usually rectangular, though earlier sanctuaries were often circular in shape. Kivas often contain carved wooden figures called kachinas (kah CHEE nuhz), which represent spirits that came from the underworld with the Hopi. Kivas also have pits for ceremonial fires.

ROLE OF WATER

Water in most mythical traditions symbolizes what some psychologists call the Unconscious, the hidden reaches of the mind where powerful energies inspire dreams, creativity, intuition, and spiritual longing. Rivers in myths often symbolize journeys into this mysterious region of the mind.

COCHIN AND

The Acoma Pueblo Indians tell this story to explain why the seasons change.

An Acoma woman named Co-chin-ne-na-ko, or Cochin for short, married Shakok, the Spirit of Winter. After the marriage, the Acoma noticed that the weather grew colder with each passing year. Corn could no longer grow. The people had only cactus leaves and other wild plants to eat.

One day, while Cochin was out gathering cactus leaves, a young man approached her. He wore a yellow shirt of corn silk, a belt, and a tall, pointed hat. His leggings and moccasins were richly decorated with sewn flowers and butterflies.

"What are you eating?" the young man asked Cochin. "Our people are starving. We must eat these cactus leaves," Cochin replied.

"Here," the young man said. "Eat this ear of corn while I fetch you more to bring home with you."

He trotted away and soon returned with a large bundle of corn. "Where did you get all this corn?" Cochin exclaimed.

MIOCHIN

"From my home, way down south," the young man replied.

"I would love to see your home! Would you take me there?" Cochin asked.

"I do not think Shakok would be pleased if I took his wife home with me," said the man.

"But I do not love him," Cochin said. "He is so cold! Ever since he came, no corn or flowers grow. We eat nothing but cactus leaves."

"Meet me here tomorrow," the man said and left.

Cochin's father and mother were amazed when she brought home an armload of corn. She told them in detail everything that had happened. "You met Miochin (mee OH shin), the Spirit of Summer," her father said. "Bring him back to the village tomorrow."

The next day, Cochin returned with Miochin and big bundles of corn. For once, everyone in the village had enough to eat. Miochin was welcome in the chief's house.

Just then, Shakok returned from the north, where he had been playing with the sleet, hail, and snow. Seeing corn, Shakok knew Miochin must be about.

"Ha, Miochin, are you there? I will destroy you!" he yelled.

"Ha, Shakok, I will destroy you!" Miochin retorted.

"Meet me here in four days," Shakok shouted. "We will fight and the victor will have Cochin as his wife!"

When the day came, Shakok roared down from the north in a terrible black cloud, bringing the ice, snow, sleet, and the winter animals with him. Miochin and his army of insects, birds, and summer animals approached in great clouds of smoke and steam from the south. Miochin and Shakok and their armies clashed, but soon Shakok was forced to fall back before the heat of the south.

The two enemies met. "You win, Miochin! Cochin is yours forever!" Shakok grumbled. But to keep the peace, they agreed that each would rule the land for half the year. Shakok would rule during winter. Miochin would rule during the summer. This is why we have a cold season for half the year and a warm season for the other half.

The World of
THE PUEBLO INDIANS

The Acoma are one of 21 federally recognized tribes of Pueblo (PWEHB loh) Indians. The Acoma and several other Pueblo groups live in New Mexico. Most, however, live in villages that lie along the Rio Grande in areas between Taos and Albuquerque in Arizona.

The Pueblo are the descendants of people sometimes called the Anasazi. In about A.D. 900, the Anasazi began establishing communities of multistory buildings, such as this dwelling (right) known as the Cliff Palace at Mesa Verde National Park in Colorado.

Pueblo is a Spanish word meaning *town*. Because several Native American tribes were living in towns when the Spaniards first came upon them in the 1500's, the Spaniards called them Pueblo Indians. Pueblo villages consisted of stone or *adobe* (sun-dried brick) structures that resembled apartment buildings. Such homes could have as many as four stories, and the Indians used ladders to reach the upper levels. Some families of grandparents, parents, children, aunts, and uncles lived in two or more connected dwellings.

MYTHS AND THE SEASONS

Myths explaining the seasons can be found in cultural traditions throughout the world. The ancient Greek story of Demeter (dih MEE tuhr) and Persephone (puhr SEHF uh nee) also gives an explanation as to why there is a warm season and a cold season. Persephone is the daugher of Demeter, the goddess of the harvest. Hades (HAY deez), the king of the Underworld, kidnaps Persephone. Eventually, Demeter agrees that her daughter will spend six months of each year with Hades. In those months, Demeter sorrows for her daughter and Earth experiences winter.

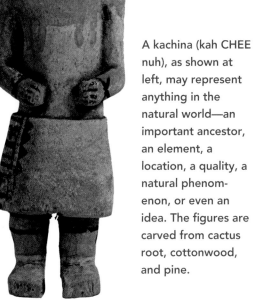

A kachina (kah CHEE nuh), as shown at left, may represent anything in the natural world—an important ancestor, an element, a location, a quality, a natural phenom-enon, or even an idea. The figures are carved from cactus root, cottonwood, and pine.

A woman of the Acoma Pueblo of New Mexico bakes bread in a traditional beehive-shaped oven built from adobe, in an illustration from the early 1900's. A number of families shared each oven. The Pueblo made their bread with flour from the corn they grew.

KIVAS AND KACHINAS

Many Pueblo religious ceremonies held in kivas are associated with the kachina belief system. During these ceremonies, masked dancers seem to become the kachinas. After the ceremonies, Hopi children are given kachinas as educational toys to help them learn about these spirits.

OLD-SALT-WOMAN
Is Refused Food

For the Cochiti Pueblo, this story explained the origin of a sacred salty lake and the importance of salt in their daily lives.

Old-Salt-Woman and her grandson were terribly poor. They came to Cochiti Pueblo (KOH chee tee PWEHB loh) and begged for something to eat. But the people were too busy cooking for a festival, and so Old-Salt-Woman and her grandson were turned away.

Outside the pueblo, at the place where all the children play, Old-Salt-Woman sat and took out a crystal. The children gathered round to see the magical object she had in her hand.

"Each of you, grab a branch of the pinion tree over there and swing yourselves." And so they did. With her magic crystal, Old-Salt-Woman turned the children into birds called Chaparral (chap uh RAL) Jays. "When we were in the pueblo, nobody invited us to stay. From now on you will be Chaparral Jays."

Old-Salt-Woman and her grandson went south to another settlement called Kewa Pueblo (KAY wah PWEHB loh). The people treated them well and fed them. When they left, Old-Salt-Woman said, "We are grateful for your hospitality." She gave them some of her own flesh to eat. The people put it on their bread and meat, and the food tasted better. It tasted salty.

"The people of Cochiti treated us badly, and so I turned their children into birds.

But you have treated us kindly. So remember if you put my flesh on your food, it will taste more delicious. We are going southwest now. If you want more of my flesh, you will find it there. When you come to find it, let there be no laughing or singing. Be quiet and clean."

Old-Salt-Woman left Kewa Pueblo and went to a great lake filled with salty water. That is why the people still travel to that lake to get their salt.

The World of **OLD-SALT-WOMAN**

The Cochiti (KOH chee tee) and Kewa (KAY wah) pueblos remain vibrant communities with rich cultural lives today. Kewa Pueblo is also known as Santo Domingo Pueblo. Both pueblos lie north of Albuquerque, New Mexico, in the southwestern United States.

GODS IN DISGUISE

Most mythic traditions feature stories of gods who wear disguises to walk among humans. The Norse god Odin walked about in a cloak and large hat. The Roman gods Jupiter and Hermes disguised themselves as poor beggars and discovered that only an old married couple, Baucis (BAW sihs) and Philemon (fuh LEE muhn), would welcome them. The Hebrew Bible warns people to show hospitality to strangers because "some have entertained angels without knowing it." In many cases, the gods come to Earth to test the goodness of humans toward society's most vulnerable members.

The poppy (left) is one of many plants of the American Southwest used in traditional Native American medicine. The poppy, as well as willow and yarrow brewed in tea, were used to treat headache, cramps, fevers, and toothache. Even the dandelion had medicinal use, in helping digestion and as a treatment for gall bladder and liver problems. Aloe is still used by many people to treat burns.

Cone-shaped rock formations, called tent rocks, or hoodoos, cluster in Kasha Katuwe Tent Rocks National Monument near Cochiti Pueblo. The tent rocks were created by volcanic eruptions 6 million to 7 million years ago.

Before refrigeration, salt was used to preserve meat and other perishable foods. Salt in the diet helps prevent *dehydration* (lack of water). Salt was also used in religious offerings, as a *disinfectant* (a substance that kills germs), and as payment for goods and services. Our modern word *salary* derives from the Latin world for salt.

Corn, beans, and squash are often referred to as "the three sisters" because the plants help one another grow. Beans provide the soil with nitrogen, which fertilizes corn. Squash is a spreading plant that provides moisture-trapping groundcover. These plants were basic crops for peoples throughout what are now the American Southwest and Mexico. Native American farmers supplemented their diet by hunting for wild game and catching fish. Later, after the Europeans introduced cattle, some tribes took up ranching.

NAYENEZGANI SLAYS THE MONSTERS

The Navajo who live in the Four Corners region—where the modern-day U.S. states of Arizona, New Mexico, Colorado, and Utah meet—tell this myth to explain the often-dangerous environment in which they live and how the gods looked after and protected the people.

In the first days, called the Anáye (ahn ah yee), the Stranger Gods nearly destroyed the human race. When only four humans remained, the Yéi (yeh ee), the Navajo Holy Ones, created two sisters, White-Shell-Woman and Changing-Woman. They each gave birth to a son. One was called Tobadzischini (also known as Born-from-Water). The other was Nayenezgani (also known as Slayer-of-the-Stranger-Gods). Sun was their father.

When the boys became men, they went to find their father. They discovered smoke rising from an underground dwelling and entered the home. Grandmother-Spider greeted them.

"Perhaps you seek the way to your father's house," observed Grandmother-Spider.

"Yes," replied Nayenezgani. "If only we knew the way."

Wise Grandmother-Spider explained the way would be hard. They would meet the Stranger Gods: the Rocks-that-

Crush, the Reeds-that-Cut, the Cactuses-that-Tear, and the Sands-that-Boil. She gave the brothers feathers from a living eagle to protect them and taught them sacred words to recite. The brothers passed by the Stranger Gods safely, reciting the words she had taught them.

At first, Sun was not happy to see his sons. He attempted to crush them against the walls of his house. He tried to burn them up in a sweat lodge. He tried to kill them with a sacred pipe filled with poisoned tobacco. But the boys held tightly to the life-feathers Grandmother-Spider had given them and survived.

Seeing their courage, Sun knew these were his sons. "Why do you seek me? Sun asked.

"Oh, father!" the boys cried. "In the place we live, the Stranger Gods have nearly devoured all the people. We want weapons so we can destroy our enemies!"

Sun gave them clothing made of knife iron, lightning arrows, and a stone knife. He took them to the Sky Hole at the top of the sky and sent them back to Earth by lightning bolt.

As soon as they returned, they heard the thunderous footsteps of the Stranger God, Yeisto, the giant. Nayenezgani shot the lightning arrows at the giant, knocking him this way and that. At last, Yeisto fell on his face and died.

The next day, Nayenezgani traveled to the land of the *Anáye* seeking the Téelget, the enormous four-footed beast with horns like a deer. Nayenezgani followed Groundhog's tunnel until he was just below the monster's heart and then loosed a lightning arrow. The beast reared up and tried to dig Nayenezgani out of the ground with his horns. But the beast's heart burst, and he died.

Day after day, Nayenezgani returned to the land of the *Anáye*. He killed the terrible Winged Creatures, transforming their ugly children into a powerful eagle and a wise owl. With one of the eagle's feathers, Nayenezgani made all the other birds on Earth. He killed He-Who-Kicks-People-Down-the-Cliff by clubbing him with his stone ax.

He also killed the People-Who-Slay-with-Their-Eyes, Bear-That-Pursues, and Traveling-Stone as well. Each time, he made something beautiful or useful from a part of the monster or one of its children.

In this way, Nayenezgani made the world safer for people to live in.

The World of
THE NAVAJO

The Navajo (NAV uh hoh) are one of the largest Indian tribes in the United States. The Navajo reservation, which covers parts of the states of Arizona, New Mexico, and Utah, is the nation's biggest reservation. The Navajo call themselves the Diné (dih nay), meaning *the people.*

A Navajo woman stands before her hogan, a traditional dome-topped dwelling. For much of their history, the Navajo moved around during the year to graze their livestock and gather food from the wild. They built hogans from wooden poles and brushwood covered with a layer of mud. The Navajo believe the beaver people instructed Coyote to help First Man and First Woman build their own hogans. Hogans for men are square or cone-shaped; hogans for women have eight sides. The single doorway always faces east, toward the rising sun. In Navajo belief, nothing evil comes from the east, only good.

NAYENEZGANI'S BIRTH

Nayenezgani is the son of Changing-Woman. One morning, Changing-Woman lay on a rock, her feet pointed east. The rising sun touched her. That same morning White-Shell-Woman sat under a waterfall. Four days later, the sisters felt life moving within them. Four days after that, Changing-Woman gave birth to Nayenezgani, and White-Shell-Woman gave birth to Tobadzischini. The two cousins are described as brothers in the stories about them.

Navajo women herd their sheep in Canyon de Chelly in Arizona. Livestock farming remains important to the Navajo economy.

A Navajo weaver sits before her loom in her hogan. The Navajo are expert weavers. They traditionally wove their own clothes and blankets, but for 150 years they have also woven items to sell to tourists. Navajo textiles have strong geometric patterns in brown, white, black, yellow, red, and gray. The yarn is dyed using such natural materials as indigo (blue), rabbit brush plant (yellow), and *cochineal* (scale insects, for red). Weavers use an upright loom, which, according to legend, the first Navajo women learned how to make from Spider-Woman, whose loom used parts of the sky, the rays of the sun, and lightning.

A Navajo rug depicts nine spirits called *Yéi (yeh ee)*. Yéi can be kind and helpful, like the Holy People whom the Navajo associate with such forces of nature as the wind or the rain. But the Yéi can also be monstrous demons. The Navajo worship the Yéi in night-time ceremonies in which dancers wear masks to represent the gods.

The Sacrifice Of
COCIJO

The Zapotec Indians of what is now southern Mexico told this myth to explain the origin of fire.

Pitao (PEE tow), the uncreated Father-of-the-Gods, created the heavens, sun, moon, stars, Earth, seasons, animals, plants, rivers, lakes, and seas in a single exhalation of his mighty breath. He gathered the lesser gods together and gave each of them power over particular elements of his creation.

But he gave no power to Cocijo (koh SEE hoh), for he was the smallest of the gods and was given little respect. After establishing the Order of Things, Pitao created human beings, who multiplied until they covered the land in all directions. They were the Zapotec (ZAH puh tehk), the chosen people of Pitao.

However, one element of creation was missing. Pitao had not

created fire. He had not done so because he wished to see how hard the people would work and to test the spirit of sacrifice among the lesser gods.

At night, without the warmth of the sun, the people shivered with cold. The birds burrowed deep into vegetation, and the animals looked for shelter in caves and burrows to keep from freezing.

Seeing that there was no fire and that Pitao, the uncreated Father-of-the-Gods, seemed indifferent to their plight, the people decided to build a mound as tall as a mountain. From this high mound, they hoped, their prayers could be more easily heard in heaven, and Pitao would take pity on them.

And so every night and every day they piled up stones and dirt without ceasing. People came from all over Earth to labor, like so many ants. After many suns and many moons, the people succeeded. Their mound was indeed as tall as a mountain. Upon this mound they built a pyramid dedicated to Pitao. When they had finished, they returned to the bottom of the mound to wait.

Pitao, moved by the people's devotion, decided at last to create fire. He gathered the gods at the top of the mound. There, the uncreated Father-of-the-Gods had stacked an enormous pile of wood. He rubbed two sticks together. He kept rubbing until flames burst forth, igniting the woodpile.

"My children," said Pitao to the gods. "Now comes the test of devotion. Whichever one of you sacrifices his sacred body in the flames shall receive everlasting honor."

The first to attempt the test was the God-of-Waters. He ran to the flames, but they were too hot, and so the god shrank back, ashamed. The God-of-the-Harvest, made the next attempt. But, racing up to the flames, he was turned back by their intense heat and returned to his place, ashamed. The God-of-Hunting and Fishing also tried, but with no better result.

After some time, only Cocijo, the smallest of the gods, had not tested the flames. Pitao did not think it even worth suggesting that he do so. But Cocijo begged Pitao for the chance, and when the other gods turned to see what the Father-of-the-Gods would do, he said, "Test it."

Cocijo begged his brother the God-of-Waters to soak him. He pleaded with the God-of-Winds to blow the flames back a bit. Once they did, Cocijo threw himself headlong into the flames without hesitation. The hungry flames leapt higher. An enormous black cloud rose above the great mound, towering to the heavens.

Suddenly, great flashes of lightning appeared in the cloud. They were so bright that both gods and people were blinded temporarily. The ends of Earth were lit up, and an enormous thunderclap nearly froze the hearts of both people and beasts.

The people, having overcome their fear, cried out, "We have fire! We have fire! Thank you, Pitao!"

In exchange for this sacrifice, Pitao named Cocijo the ruler of all the other gods. The Zapotec named the great mound the Hill of Flame and paid homage to it as the Sacred Hill of the Dead, the place where Cocijo's body is buried.

The World of THE ZAPOTEC

The Zapotec (ZAH puh tehk) developed an empire in what is now the state of Oaxaca (wah HAH kuh) in southern Mexico from about 1500 B.C. to A.D. 750. Their capital city, known today as Monte Alban, had a ceremonial district that included temples and a ball court.

A carved stone head with an elaborate headdress from a building in Monte Alban may represent the ruler of a province controlled by the Zapotec empire.

The artistry of the Zapotec is vividly displayed in a 1945 mural by Mexican artist Diego Rivera. The mural shows Indians panning for gold ore in a river (top) and processing the ore in a foundry (right). Artists skillfully use the gold and feathers from native birds to create extravagent headdresses for warriors or nobles (middle, left).

Zapotec pyramids were among the earliest built in the Americas. These square, four-sided structures rose in a series of steps to a flat top.

THE SACRIFICE OF COCIJO

Cocijo's (koh SEE hohz) willingness to sacrifice himself for the good of humans makes him the ruler of all the gods. Other cultures tell similar stories of gods who sacrifice themselves so that humankind will benefit. In return for this sacrifice, the Zapotec may have included human sacrifices to the gods during their religious rituals. For later peoples of Mexico, particularly the Aztec, the sacrifice of humans became a central part of their religion. They believed it was essential in order to show thanks for the sacrifices the gods themselves had made on behalf of others.

A section of a Zapotec manuscript includes images of gods, people, and animals. The Zapotec developed a writing system that used a separate *glyph* (symbol) to represent each syllable of the language. Scholars believe the Zapotec inspired the Aztec and Maya to create their own writing systems.

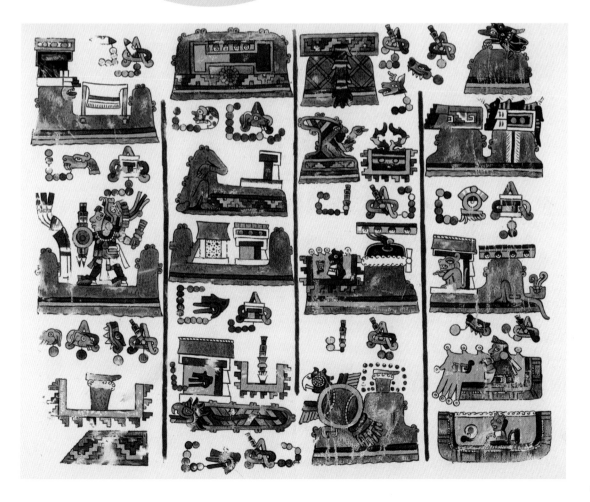

The Creation of
EARTH

The Aztec told this myth to explain how Earth came to be.

When the world was still dark, only our Grandmother–Grandfather, Ometeotl (oh meht tee AH tul), existed. From within Ometeotl came four mighty ones: Huitzilopochtli (wee tsee loh PAHCH tlee—south), Quetzalcoatl (keht sahl koh WAH tuhl—east), Tezcatlipoca (tehs kah tlee POH kah—west), and Xipe Totec (SHEE pay TOH tehk—north). Quetzalcoatl and Huitzilopochtli then began the task of creating.

A fire appeared, a half-sun that gave little light. The first man and first woman, Oxomoco (oh shoh MOH koh) and Cipactonal (see pak TOH nahl), appeared. Next came days and divisions of time. The Underworld came into being, with its Lord and Lady to rule over it. With the help of their brothers,

Quetzalcoatl and Huitzilopochtli created the Lord and Lady of Water who covered all the Earth, which was then only a muddy ooze. The sea monster, Cipactli (see PAHK tlee), swam in the primordial waters. After a time, Cipactli created the Lord and Lady of Earth.

Lady Earth was fierce, like Cipactli. She could not be controlled. The joints of her limbs were filled with eyes and mouths, all of which bit like mad dogs.

Quetzalcoatl and Tezcatlipoca fought with Lady Earth. They grabbed her arms and legs and pulled until she tore in half.

The killing displeased the other gods. To make up for it, Quetzalcoatl and Tezcatlipoca used the goddess's body to make all things necessary for human survival. Her hair became trees, flowers, and herbs. Her skin became the short grass and small flowers. Her countless eyes were converted into wells, fountains, and caves. Her many mouths became rivers and large caves. Her nose and shoulders became valleys and mountains. The other half of her body was used to create the starry heavens.

Today, one can still hear Lady Earth weeping at night, wanting to devour human hearts. She will not be quiet until she is fed. Nor will she produce fruit unless she is given blood to drink.

The World of THE AZTEC

The Aztec were an American Indian people who ruled a mighty empire in what is now Mexico during the 1400's and early 1500's.

According to legend, the Aztec left their homeland and traveled until they saw an eagle eating a snake perched on a blooming cactus. There, in A.D. 1325, in the Valley of Mexico, they founded the city of Tenochtitlan (tay nohch TEE tlahn) in the middle of marshy Lake Texcoco (TEHK KOH koh).

Quetzalcoatl (keht sahl koh WAH tuhl, right), whose name means Feathered Serpent, was a major Aztec deity. He is associated in myth with wind, the planet Venus, the dawn, merchants, and arts and crafts. He was also the patron god of Aztec priests and of learning. Almost every Indian civilization in Mexico worshiped Quetzalcoatl.

Aztec priests cut the beating heart from a young man in a sacrifice to the un, in an image from an Aztec *codex* (historical manuscript) from the 1500's. Human sacrifice lay at the center of most major Aztec religious ceremonies. A sacrifice was a dramatic and shocking event, which was probably intended to show the power of the gods and the emperor. The victim was taken to a temple, which was on a pyramid at the top of a steep flight of steps. The priests laid the person on a special stone, cut open his or her chest with a special knife (above), and pulled out the heart. Then the victim was rolled down the steps to the ground.

SACRED EMPERORS

One of the most important roles of Aztec myths is to underline the status of the elite who ruled Aztec society. Aztec emperors were often described as divine rulers who were closely connected to the supernatural world of the gods and goddesses. One of the emperor's duties was to make sure that events and rituals took place according to the Aztec calendar, which predicted future events. The Aztec believed that time repeated itself in cycles. They saw such events as births, deaths, and wars as re-enactments of events from myths.

Buildings erected by Spaniards surround the ruins of the Aztec temple known as the Templo Mayor (Great Temple) in Mexico City. After the Spaniards conquered the Aztec in 1521, they destroyed and built over much of Tenochtitlan, the Aztec capital, in an effort to replace the native culture with their own Christian culture.

The Birth of
HUITZILOPOCHTLI

The Aztec told this story to explain the origin of war in their culture.

Coatlicue (koh aht LEE kway—Woman-with-the-Serpent-Skirt) gave birth to 400 star gods of the south and a daughter, Coyolxauhqui (koh yohl SHAH kee). Later, Coatlicue felt growing within her a son, Huitzilopochtli (wee tsee loh PAHCH tlee), also known as Hummingbird-From-the-Left. This enraged Coyolxauhqui and her 400 star brothers, so they waged war against their mother.

When Coatlicue heard that her own children were coming to kill her, she became very frightened and sad. But, coming from within her womb, she heard the voice of Huitzilopochtli. He said, "Do not fear, mother. I know what I must do." The god's words comforted Coatlicue.

In the south, the 400 star brothers prepared for war. They twisted and bound up their long hair as warriors do. They put on warriors' clothing. They sharpened the points of their arrows. But their brother Cuahuitlicac did not agree with going to war. He ran as fast as he could to warn his mother of the star brothers' approach.

The star brothers marched in an orderly line. Their sister led them. From his post on a high mountain, Cuahuitlicac reported every stage of their journey. At last he said, "They are here. Their sister, Coyolxauhqui, leads them."

At that moment, Huitzilopochtli, the god of war, was born. Immediately, he armed himself. He put on his shield of eagle feathers and took up his darts and blue dart-thrower. He painted his face with diagonal stripes. On his head, he arranged fine feathers; he put in his earplugs. On his left foot, which was withered, he wore a sandal covered with feathers. His legs and his arms were painted blue.

Rushing into battle, Huitzilopochtli struck off his sister's head with a fire-serpent. Her body fell where she died.

Later, to console his mother, Huitzilopochtli placed Coyolxauhqui's head in the sky. It became the moon, and her mother could see it every night.

Nor did the 400 star brothers escape Huitzilopochtli's anger. He harassed them up one mountain and down another. They begged for mercy, but he would not relent. Huitzilopochtli killed them all. When he had vented his wrath, the war god took their shields, their armor, and their ornaments. Thus, Huitzilopochtli fulfilled his destiny to possess the armor and wealth of his enemies.

For this reason, the Aztecs venerated Huitzilopochtli and offered him sacrifices. And the god rewarded those who did and made them a great people.

The World of AZTEC WARRIORS

Nearly every Aztec male had to serve in the army. Boys started their military training when they were still at school. Up to the age of 10, boys had their head shaved. Once they began their training, they grew a lock of hair on the back of their head. They were not allowed to cut off this hair until they had captured a prisoner in battle. At school, boys learned how to use weapons and took part in mock battles. Then they were sent to a real war. At first, they carried equipment and helped other soldiers. Only after they had gained experience were they allowed to fight themselves.

The Tenayuca Pyramid, built by the Chichimec people in the 1200's, became the model used by the Aztecs for their own pyramids. Today, the pyramid is almost surrounded by Mexico City.

Religion was the main reason for Aztec warfare. Because the Aztec needed a steady supply of prisoners to sacrifice to the gods, warfare was vital to the survival of the Aztec. According to Aztec myth, gods were sacrificed to bring the world into being. The Aztec therefore had to repay them for this sacrifice with human blood. If they failed to make this offering, the sun might stop moving in the sky and disaster would follow.

WARRIOR CULTS

Elite Aztec warriors belonged to one of two military orders: the Eagle Warriors or the Jaguar Warriors. The two groups were the most feared Aztec soldiers and had captured many enemies in battle. The eagle was the symbol of the sun; the jaguar was the symbol of Tezcatlipoca (tehs kah tlee POH kah), the night sky. The warriors wore eagle feathers or jaguar skins in battle. They believed these objects would give them the qualities of the respective animals.

A painted clay statue shows an Eagle Warrior dressed for battle. His helmet is based on an eagle's head, complete with a beak. The statue, which stands about 5 ½ inches (170 centimeters) tall, was found at the doorway to a chamber where Eagle Warriors met.

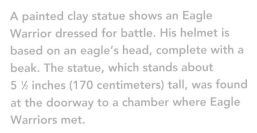

Aztec warriors carrying spears and round shields appear in an illustration from an Aztec *codex* (historical manuscript) from the 1500's. Four followers of a defeated rebellious lord (top) beg for mercy. Aztec warriors rarely tried to kill their enemies. Instead, they tried to capture them to use them as sacrifices for the gods.

The Departure of
QUETZALCOATL

For the Toltec, this myth explained the close link between the people and Quetzalcoatl. It also explained how Quetzalcoatl influenced other peoples of ancient Mexico.

The Toltec say that Tezcatlipoca (tehs kah tlee POH kah), the Dark Lord and the twin of Quetzalcoatl (keht sahl koh WAH tuhl), was a mischief-maker. He once tricked his brother and the priestess, Quetzalpetatl (keht sahl pet WAH tuhl) into becoming lovers.

The next day, Tezcatlipoca urged the people to demand Quetzalcoatl's exile from the kingdom of Tula (TOO luh). But no one felt worse about what had happened than Quetzalcoatl. He prayed to Chalchiuhtlicue (chahl chee wee TLEE kwah) (She-of-the-Jade-Skirt), seeking punishment in order that he could be purified.

Chalchiuhtlicue rebuked Quetzalcoatl saying, "Because you broke your vow, you must leave this place!" But Chalchiuhtlicue only pretended to be displeased. She knew Quetzalcoatl had to be humbled by exile to become a mediator for the people.

Quetzalcoatl wept. "I feel alone," he cried. "There is no happiness anywhere. What else can I do but die?" He lay down in a coffin, hoping to be taken from this life. When Death did not come after four days, Quetzalcoatl resolved to leave the kingdom of Tula forever.

Quetzalcoatl spoke to his followers: "We are leaving. Bury the riches we have discovered together. Make it as though our world never existed."

His people buried their silver, gold, coral, and jade. They burned the books they could not carry. At the edge of town, many people came to see them off—but Tezcatlipoca and his followers came to jeer and throw stones. Quetzalcoatl's heart was broken. At night, he climbed a rock to catch one last glimpse of Tula, his beloved city. To this day you can see his handprints on the rock. To this day you can see the holes on the top of this rock made by his tears.

For two years, Quetzalcoatl wandered from town to town. Wherever he stopped, people gathered to listen to his teachings and asked him to be their king. Instead, Quetzalcoatl left one of his followers at each city to be king in his place.

At last, he came to a town called Cholula (choh LOO lah). He stayed there and taught the people the Toltec way. This is why the Cholulans became a great people.

The World of THE TOLTEC

The Toltec (TOHL tehk) Indians established an empire in the highlands of central Mexico during the A.D. 900's. They were the dominant people in the region until 1200. The center of Toltec culture was a city known today as Tula, about 45 miles (70 kilometers) north of Mexico City. No one knows what the Toltec called themselves or their city. The Aztec later honored the Toltec as the founders of urban civilization in the highlands. The Aztec words for artisan, sage, and civilization come from their word for the Toltec.

A magnificent Toltec funerary mask was created as a mosaic with pieces of turquoise, shell, and coral. Such death masks were placed over the face of the deceased and may have been modeled on that individual's features.

END OF THE TOLTEC

During the 1100's, nomads began to cross the northern frontiers of the Toltec empire in what is now central Mexico. As these nomads settled in the Valley of Mexico, Toltec dominance ended. The invading groups included the Aztec, who gradually replaced the Toltec as the most powerful people in the Mexican highlands.

The elaborate bird headdresses on two Toltec warriors mark them as high-ranking nobles. Toltec warriors also wore shields on their back to protect their kidneys.

The god Quetzalcoatl emerges from the jaws of a coyote, which represents Earth, in a Toltec sculpture. Pieces of mother-of-pearl—a lustrous, rainbow-colored material from certain shellfish—cover the sculpture.

An artist imagines Toltec workers (top) hauling the top of one of the warrior statues, known as Atlantes, to the platform of the Pyramid of the Morning Star (bottom) in Tula, probably the Toltec capital. The Atlantes served as columns to support the roof of the temple-pyramid, which was dedicated to the god Quetzalcoatl (keht sahl koh WAH tuhl). Tula lies near the modern town of Hidalgo, Mexico.

DEITIES OF SOUTHWESTERN UNITED STATES AND MEXICO

Cinteotl

Each April, the Aztec made offerings to Cinteotl, the god of corn (maize) by cutting themselves and dripping their blood on reeds that they placed outside their homes.

Cipactli (see PAHK tlee)

The Aztec saw Cipactli as a fearsome sea monster who was part crocodile, part fish, and part toad. Cipactli was always hungry and had many mouths.

Cipactonal (see pak TOH nahl)

An Aztec god of calendars. Cipactonal and Oxomoco were said to be the first human couple.

Coatlicue (koh aht LEE kway)

The "Lady of the Serpent Skirt" was the Aztec Earth goddess and the mother of the war god Huitzilopochtli. She was the serpent goddess and was portrayed as looking hideous, with a skirt of writhing snakes.

Cochin (KOH chihn)

Also known as Co-chin-ne-na-ko, she was known to the Pueblo Indians as the woman who married Shakok, the Spirt of Winter, but who brought Miochin, the Spirit of Summer, to the people.

Cocijo (koh SEE hoh)

The Zapotec believed that Cocijo sacrificed himself in order to bring humans fire. The Zapotec saw him as the god of lightning and the creator of their world.

Coyolxauhqui (koh yohl SHAH kee)

The sister of Huitzilopochtli, Coyol-xauhqui led her 400 star brothers in a fight against Coatlicue, their mother, because she became pregnant with Huitzilopochtli, the god of war.

Coyote

Coyote appears in the myths of many North American peoples, particularly in the Southwest where wild coyotes were common. Coyote is a trickster god, who sometimes helps people but sometimes causes harm and destruction. It is often difficult to know why Coyote acts in a particular way. Native peoples believed that Coyote's mischievous behavior is one of the reasons for the troubles and problems that occur in everyday life.

Cuahuitlicac

The Aztec believed that Cuahuitlicac was one of the many sons of Coatlicue who warned his mother when his brothers and sister came to kill her. He is now one of the stars of the southern sky.

Huitzilopochtli (wee tsee loh PAHCH tlee)

The Aztec god of war presided over the major pyramid temple in Tenochtitlan and was the recipient of thousands of human sacrifices. He was seen as the sun, who was born each day and defeated the stars of night, and was the tribal god of the Aztec who guided their migration to Tenochtitlán. His name means *blue hummingbird on the left.*

Miochin (mee OH shin)

In Pueblo myth, Miochin was the Spirit of Summer, who encouraged crops to grow. He fought Shakok for the hand of Cochin and struck a deal with the Spirit of Winter to divide the year between them.

Nayenezgani

For the Navajo, Nayenezgani and his brother, Tobadzischini, were the sons of Changing-Woman and the Sun. Nayenezgani killed many monsters to make the world safer for the Navajo.

Old-Salt-Woman

For the Zuni of New Mexico, Old-Salt-Woman is both the mother of the Zuni people and a sacred lake in New Mexico that is revered by the Zuni and other Native American peoples.

Ometeotl (oh meht tee AH tul)

In Aztec myth, Ometeotl was the master of all existence who lay outside time and space and who brought together such opposites as male and female, light and dark, and order and chaos.

Oxomoco (oh shoh MOH koh)

In Aztec myth, the goddess of the night, astrology, and the calendar. Oxomoco and Cipactonal were said to be the first human couple.

Pitao (PEE tow)

To the Zapotec, Pitao was the original creator who created the universe and everything in it through his breath and later assigned the lesser gods their different areas of responsibility.

Quetzalcoatl (keht sahl koh WAH tuhl)

To the Aztec, the "Plumed Serpent" was the giver of breath and the god of winds. He was also honored as the creator of humans and as an ancient king of the Toltec who showed humans how to grow corn, how to weave textiles, and how to use the stars to follow the calendar.

Shakok

To the Acoma Pueblo, Shakok was the Spirit of Winter who married a woman from a pueblo. He spent most of the time with his people in the far north, but returned to the pueblo bringing sleet and snow.

Spider-Woman

Spider Woman features in myths of the Pueblo peoples, particularly the Hopi. She was a messenger for the Creator who taught people how to weave.

Tezcatlipoca (tehs kah tlee POH kah)

"Smoking Mirror" was an Aztec god who was the patron of warriors but who was also a trickster who constantly made trouble for his brother, Quetzalcoatl.

Tlaloc (tlah LOK)

Tlaloc was the rain god of the Toltec and was later adopted by the Aztec. He controlled clouds, rain, and lightning.

Xipe Totec (SHEE pay TOH tehk)

The Aztec saw the "Flayed Lord" as a god of agriculture and vegetation. He gave food to humans by agreeing to have himself skinned alive—in the same way the corn seed loses its skin when it begins to put out shoots.

GLOSSARY

creation The process by which the universe was brought into being.

creator In myth, a creator god is one who creates the universe or Earth, geographical features, and often all humans or a particular culture. Creation myths explain the origins of the world, but often do so by describing actions that seem to take place in a world that already exists.

cult A system of religious devotion based on a particular individual or object.

irrigation The provision of a regular supply of water to an area of land in order to allow crops to grow.

kachina In Pueblo myth, a revered ancestral spirit or the figurine who represents it.

kiva An underground or partly underground chamber used by Pueblo peoples to hold religious ceremonies.

myth A traditional story that a people tell to explain their own origins or the origins of natural and social phenomena. Myths often involve gods, spirits, and other supernatural beings.

plaza A public square or marketplace in a built-up area.

pow-wow A North American ceremony involving music and dancing.

quetzal A bird in tropical America which is valued for its iridescent green and red feathers.

ritual A solemn religious ceremony in which a set of actions are peformed in a specific order.

sacred Something that is connected with the gods or goddesses and so should be treated with respectful worship.

sacrifice An offering made to a god or gods, often in the form of an animal or even a person who is killed for the purpose. Sacrifices also take the shape of valued possessions that might be buried, placed in caves, or thrown into a lake for the gods.

Snake Ceremony A Hopi ceremony held every two years to pray for rain. Dancers carry snakes in their mouths that they believe will carry their prayers to the Rainmakers beneath Earth.

shaman A person who enters a trance during a religious ritual in order to gain access to the world of the spirits; in many cultures, a shaman is seen as an intermediary between humans and the spiritual world.

supernatural Describes something that cannot be explained by science or by the laws of nature, which is therefore said to be caused by such beings as gods, spirits, or ghosts.

sweat lodge A dome-shaped hut used for ritual steam baths as a form of purification.

tipi A conical tent made from animal skins covering a frame of wooden poles.

trickster A supernatural figure who engages in mischievous activities that either benefit or harm humans. The motives behind a trickster's behavior are not always clear. Tricksters appear in various shapes in myths around the world, including Coyote and Raven in Native American cultures and Anansi the spider in West Africa.

turquoise A pale blue-green mineral valued for the purity of its color and used by many Native American people to make jewelry.

FOR FURTHER INFORMATION

Books

Bingham, Ann. *South and Meso-American Mythology A to Z* (Mythology A to Z Series). Facts on File, 2004.

Dalal, Anita. *Mesoamerican Myths* (Myths from Around the World). Gareth Stevens Publishing, 2010.

Hyde, Natalie. *Understanding Mesoamerican Myths* (Myths from Around the World). Crabtree Publishing, 2013.

Kopp, Megan. *Understanding Native American Myths* (Myths Understood). Crabtree Publishing Company, 2013.

Lowenstein, Tom, and Piers Vitebsky. *Native American Myths and Beliefs* (World Mythologies). Rosen Publishing Group, 2012.

National Geographic Essential Visual History of World Mythology. National Geographic Society, 2008.

Ollhoff, Jim. *Mayan and Aztec Mythology* (The World of Mythology). ABDO Publishing Company, 2012.

Oughton, Jennie, and Lisa Desimini. *How the Stars Fell Into the Sky: A Navajo Legend.* Paw Prints, 2009.

Philip, Neil. *Eyewitness Mythology* (DK Eyewitness Books). DK Publishing, 2011.

Schomp, Virginia. *The Aztecs* (Myths of the World). Marshall Cavendish Benchmark, 2009.

Schomp, Virginia. *The Native Americans* (Myths of the World). Marshall Cavendish Benchmark, 2008.

West, David, et al. *Mesoamerican Myths* (Graphic Mythology). Rosen Publishing Group, 2006.

Yasuda, Anita, and Mark Pennington. *Warrior Twins: A Navajo Hero Myth* (Short Tales Native American Myths). Magic Wagon, 2012.

Zimmerman, Larry J. *Exploring the Life, Myth, and Art of Native Americans* (Civilizations of the World). Rosen Publishing Group, 2009.

Websites

http://www.godchecker.com/pantheon/native-american-mythology.php
A directory of Native American deities from God Checker, written in a light-hearted style but with accurate information.

http://www.godchecker.com/pantheon/aztec-mythology.php
The God Checker index of Aztec deities, with links to individual entries.

http://www.pantheon.org/areas/mythology/americas/
Encyclopedia Mythica page with links to many pages about myths from different American cultures.

http://www.crystalinks.com/aztecgods.html
This Crystal Links collection has a number of entries about Aztec gods.

http://www.mythencyclopedia.com/Ar-Be/Aztec-Mythology.html
Myth Encyclopedia entry on Aztec mythology.

http://www.native-languages.org/pueblo-legends.htm
A page with links to Pueblo myths and articles about the Pueblo.

INDEX

PRONUNCIATION KEY

Sound	As in
a	hat, map
ah	father, far
ai	care, air
aw	order
aw	all
ay	age, face
ch	child, much
ee	equal, see
ee	machine, city
eh	let, best
ih	it, pin, hymn
k	coat, look
o	hot, rock
oh	open, go
oh	grow, tableau
oo	rule, move, food
ow	house, out
oy	oil, voice
s	say, nice
sh	she, abolition
u	full, put
u	wood
uh	cup, butter
uh	flood
uh	about, ameba
uh	taken, purple
uh	pencil
uh	lemon
uh	circus
uh	labyrinth
uh	curtain
uh	Egyptian
uh	section
uh	fabulous
ur	term, learn, sir, work
y	icon, ice, five
yoo	music
zh	pleasure